Z. D. GARNER

Z. D. Garner

ISBN:
978-1-984-17158-0

Part One

Dispute of the Times

Chapter One

November 1808

"It is absolutely preposterous."

The elderly woman shook her head continuously to emphasize her point. On top of her head bounced hair having the dirty appearance of snow pushed aside by carriages on a busy Vienna road. The voice raised next was one of reason.

"You cannot conclude that Herr Beethoven himself is a barbarian. Despite whom he dedicates his music to, he is still the most brilliant in all of Vienna."

The tall stature of the speaker drew the eyes of his audience upward in a way that made the man appear superior. He was perfectly groomed, from the slickness of his hair to the smooth fit of his clothing. His daughter, Elizabeth, sat poised beside him, quiet, as she observed the conversation going on in the room. A robust man with an accurately tailored coat challenged the comment.

"A man who has the audacity to dedicate his work of music to that beast, the so-called 'Emperor of France,' is no man who deserves the respect of the public. Aside from the fact that his music is far too rambunctious to be performed for the élite of Vienna."

Elizabeth cocked her head curiously at the accusation. In the few months that she and her father had lived in Vienna, she had heard about the famous Viennese piano virtuoso,

Ludwig von Beethoven. She knew of his talent and success as a composer and performer, and even about his rough personality, but she had yet to hear him perform.

"He is a brute of a man," the elderly woman scolded, her voice shaking as she spoke. "It is evident in both his music and personality alike."

"He revoked his dedication to Bonaparte – that must redeem his reputation," a burly man with a booming voice spoke as he rose from his seat. The brown hat he wore cast a shadow over his brow, giving him a grim facial expression.

"That does not excuse the fact he admires a man who imposes chaos upon our streets as well as throughout the rest of Europe," another man in the room argued.

The room filled with the loud sound of

multiple voices as the argument become unmanageable. Nicholas leaned over to Elizabeth with his hand cupped around his mouth.

"Shall we leave?" he said to her, not really asking, but suggesting that they seize the moment to escape. The two stood and briskly left the salon.

The light of sunset bled onto the street in streaks of red and deep orange. Elizabeth followed her father into the black carriage waiting for them, being mindful to hold up her skirt to avoid tripping over it. Nicholas turned to her and spoke.

"I was disappointed to see that Karl and Maximilian were unable to attend. Karl always has such intelligent input and I was hopeful that you would be able to become better acquainted with Maximilian."

Elizabeth grimaced at the latter comment. She had known Max since they were very young, although as children they were never close friends. Their fathers had a strong friendship and wished to join the families with the marriage of their children. While Max was not an unsuitable match, Elizabeth felt no connection to him on an emotional level. Even so, she knew the expectations of the élite and of her father.

"I have heard so many contradictory proclamations," Elizabeth said, eagerly changing the subject. "I would like to experience Herr Beethoven's music for myself."

"The premiere of his fifth symphony is in December at the Theater an der Wien. I can get us tickets to the performance, if you would like."

"That would be extraordinary."

"Consider it done."

Chapter Two

December 1808

The music hall bustles with the chatter of the audience and the sounds of warm-up from the orchestra, organized on the stage in a semi circle. On cue, the concertmaster glides to his spot at the front of the violin section. The orchestra ceases to play. The concertmaster slides his bow across the instrument in his arms, creating a vibration on the string that sends the tuning note out into the space of the vast hall. The rest of the orchestra follows suit and plays the same note, tuning their instruments individually until each is perfectly matched to the other. Then, the orchestra is silent.

A repetitive smacking of heel on wood brings the attention of the entire room to meet on a single individual. Wearing a suit with tails and a sour expression, the man walks across the stage with a persistent stride that sends his coat tails flapping behind him. Clapping erupts from the audience as they welcome the conductor onto the stage. Thousands of eyes gaze in awe as he takes position at the center. Turning his back to the audience, he raises his arms to signal to the orchestra. Upright and prepared to begin, the players anticipate the cue of the conductor. At the fall of his arms, the hall erupts with melodic chords that begin the performance.

~~~

The large sound of the music washed over Elizabeth in waves. She was familiar with the structure of symphonies, as were all the élite in Vienna. Yet, there was something about this music that was different to her ear. It moved in a different direction than Mozart or Salieri pieces. It had its own agenda.

Elizabeth was intrigued by the change, involuntarily drawn to the sound of the unexpected dynamics and chords. She watched the man on the stage waving his arms, signaling entrances and cut offs to the performers. His hair was longer than that of most and curled at the edges of his neck. The arms of his jacket creased deeply in an effort to keep up with the pace of his swing. At each downbeat, a new sound rang out.

The symphony ended with an abundance of loud crashing chords that kept Elizabeth on the edge of her seat. She placed a hand on her chest, feeling the beat of her heart echo the vibrations of the orchestra. Hands held high in the air, Beethoven appeared as though he were releasing the sound into the empty space above in the way that wedding doves are released to commemorate a marriage.

As the curtains drew closed, Elizabeth grabbed the arm of her father, who was sitting next to her.

"This performance was splendid, Papa. The melodic structure of the first movement is truly stunning," she said, her voice raised in excitement.

"Indeed," Nicholas replied, keeping his voice hushed. "Although the harmony is a smidge robust for my taste."

"I rather admire the loud tones," Elizabeth argued matter-of-factly. "Not to mention how involved the conductor was. It was almost as if he himself was performing."

"It is quite impressive for a man who is nearly deaf," he said, nodding as he did so.

"That's impossible. How could a man who

is nearly deaf conduct music he can hardly hear?"

"Fortunately, he is the composer. I would be surprised if he couldn't conduct the symphony with his eyes closed."

The pair followed the bustle of people out onto the street, the line shuffling along at a slow pace.

"Elizabeth, do you know why I brought you here tonight?" Nicholas asked his daughter.

"I did not think there was a specific reason, save to come enjoy a performance."

"There was a reason, in fact. I have noticed that you have grown out of your mother's lessons; you need a much more advanced teacher."

"What does tonight's performance have in

this? Shall I be taking lessons from one of the performers? They are all very talented."

"No, I had a much grander idea in mind. I have asked Herr Beethoven to take you on as a student. It would be a challenge for you, but being as he is the most talented pianist in all Vienna, I am sure he will have infinite teachings for you."

Elizabeth's face brightened. The shade of pink in her cheeks grew darker as her smile tightened fiercely.

"Papa! This is the most wonderful news." Her voice was almost shrill and he shushed her to avoid the attention of the crowd around them. "When do I begin?"

"Do not get your hopes up just yet, he has not agreed to it. However, I have invited him to our Christmas dinner party and I am hoping that will help to sway his answer."

"Then we shall see very soon, now, won't we," Elizabeth said with a laugh.

Chapter Three

December 1808

Elizabeth was poised on a short stool with a three-pane mirror on the vanity before her. Her handmaiden, Mariana, was pinning the long curls of her hair up. She decorated the bun with pins encrusted with diamonds and rubies, a simple embellishment that matched the crimson velvet dress that hung in the armoire, anticipating its filling.

Smiling in the mirror, Elizabeth watched Mariana working. From the jewelry box on the dresser, Mariana lifted up a necklace with similar decorations to the hairpins. A glossy central ruby was surrounded by a multitude of shining diamonds that played with the light of the candles on the counter. Hung across her collarbones, the necklace was as heavy as it looked to be. Returning to the dresser, Mariana pulled out matching earrings of the same kind.

"Are you excited for the arrival of Herr Beethoven tonight, Elise?" Marina asked.

"Indeed I am," Elizabeth answered. "How lucky am I to meet a man of such talent? I may even try to dance with him."

"You don't suppose this will make Maximilian jealous?"

"I could care less what that pompous fool thinks," Elizabeth said. "He is not in charge of me and I plan to keep it that way."

"Your father will not be pleased with your

refusal to marry Max."

"Father will come around someday. His loyalty to General Wahs makes him blind to the true nature of Maximilian Wahs."

Mariana pulled a dress delicately from the armoire and unfastened the back buttons. Elizabeth stepped inside the puffy skirt and held still while Mariana did up the back.

"I hope that Maximilian keeps his hands to himself this year. Last year, the wine gave his hands freedom and his loins adrenaline. I would appreciate the personal space."

"One can only hope, my lady," Mariana said, holding open the door for Elizabeth as she left the room.

~~~

In the dining room of the Braun estate, Nicholas watched the servants at work. The long mahogany dining table had been set, draped with a white satin cloth embroidered with the green leaves and red circular berries of holly. The footman was bringing out the family's best china, a copious set that had been hand-decorated in Germany.

The maids were up on ladders near the windows, drawing the tops of the drapes so that the snowfall could be seen through the windows. The candles of the three chandeliers that crossed the room were lit, and the flames allowed the crystals of the enormous structures to twinkle magnificently.

Once the plates had been arranged properly along the table, the butler distributed the place cards to their assigned positions. The card that read "Nicholas Braun" was at the head.

The West doors were opened and

Elizabeth strolled into the room. Her velvet dress swished around her legs and dragged on the floor. A few curls strayed from the rest of her pinned up hair, bouncing in tight ringlets along her hairline. She smiled as her eyes found her father and she moved to stand beside him.

"It's beautiful, father," she said, letting her eyes wander around the room at the bright decorations.

"Not unlike you, Elise." He smiled under his mustache. "That dress is very befitting."

"Thank you."

Elise sauntered up to the long table and peered over the high backed chairs at the name cards placed on the platters. She spotted Beethoven's card first, around the middle of the table. She continued to circle around, hoping to find her name nearby. She found hers at the end of the table, near the head, right next to a card reading 'Maximilian Wahs.'

"We should retire to the drawing room now, Elise," Nicholas said, motioning toward the doors to his left. "Our guests will be arriving shortly."

"I will be there momentarily," she replied. "I want to look at something."

She watched him leave and waited for the door to shut before she plucked her name card up and moved it to the middle of the table. She put her place card onto the platter that had originally been saved for Veronica Bels, the seat directly across from Beethoven. She moved Veronica's name to the empty place near the head of the table and departed the dining room, smiling to herself.

~~~

As the guests entered the drawing room after being welcomed into the house, Elizabeth anticipated every face that paraded in would belong to the musician. Facing a multitude of disappointments, she decided to socialize amongst the guests to pass the time. Elizabeth noticed a royal blue dress out of the corner of her eye and approached the wearer.

"Good evening, Maria," Elizabeth said, taking the other woman's gloved hand. "And Merry Christmas."

"To you as well, my dear Elise. That dress of yours is absolutely stunning."

"Thank you. Your blue dress really brings out the sparkles in your eyes."

"Speaking of sparkles, your eyes are positively twinkling. You have something to tell me."

"I do," Elizabeth said, hushing her voice. "Father has invited Ludwig von Beethoven to attend tonight."

"The musician?"

"Yes." Elizabeth leaned close to her friend's ear. "I'm curious to know what he is like in person."

Just as she finished her sentence, Elizabeth happened to look towards the door of the drawing room. The last guest to arrive was wearing full dinner attire with a sleek black jacket and crisp white shirt. His hair, recently cut short, was smoothed for the event. His face wore a gruff expression and his large eyes perused the room. His eyes moved past Elizabeth, despite her consistent gaze in his direction.

"Finally," she said under her breath with a smile. She lifted her skirt and maneuvered through the crowd of people towards the newest guest. A tug at her arm stopped her short and she broke from her trance. Turning her head, she found herself in the presence of Maximilian Wahs.

"Merry Christmas, Elise," he said kindly. "You look lovely in your dress. The color brings holiday spirit to the season."

Elizabeth nodded and tried to turn away. Maximilian grabbed her arm again.

"Wait, I wanted to ask you –" he began before being interrupted by the butler, who entered to announce that dinner was served.

Elizabeth obediently followed the bustle of guests into the dining room and away from Maximilian. Approaching the seat across from Beethoven, she outstretched her hand to the chair. A second hand fell over hers and she looked at the woman next to her. The person's black dress trailed to the floor and slimmed her already thin figure.

"Pardon me, Elise," she spoke sweetly. "But I believe this is my seat."

She indicated the place card that now read 'Veronica Bels.'

"My apologies, Lady Bels," Elizabeth stammered, trying to hide her frustration with a warm smile. *Of course,* she thought, annoyed. One of the servants must have noticed the switch and changed it back. The fabric of her gloves bunched as she balled her fists and trudged over to the seat next to Maximilian.

"There you are," Maximilian said lightly. "I was beginning to think you were lost."

He smiled widely at her and she forced a laugh in return. After sitting, she craned her neck to see the musician at the other end of the table. He was thanking the footman for the bowl of soup placed before him. The lady beside him placed her hand on his arm and began a conversation, which Elizabeth could not hear. Her cheeks grew warmer, but her father's voice drew her away from the sight.

"Elise," he began. "Robert Wahs and Max have just informed me of their recent return from Russia. Wouldn't you like to ask Max about his trip?"

"I might," she replied. "If Maximilian has anything intriguing to say about it."

"In fact I do," Maximilian chimed in.

Elizabeth hardly listened. She ignored the chattering of the man beside her, and kept her attention focused on the man at the opposite end of the table. Out of the corner of her eye she could see him laughing with the woman to his right. Elizabeth thought to herself that the woman's dress was a bit too low cut for her age.

Light pressure on her hand brought Elizabeth back to the conversation she was trying to avoid.

"I just had to come back early so that I could see you," Maximilian said, his hand resting delicately on hers. "I am so glad I did."

Startled, Elizabeth looked at her father. He was preoccupied with a separate conversation with General Wahs. Nodding his head and laughing, he rose from his seat and raised his wine class.

"A toast," he began. "To this jolly Christmas and for many fortunes to come in the New Year."

~~~

The tall ceiling of the ballroom was

adorned with pastoral colors arranged as a sky. Cherubs with curly blonde hair and fat, rosy cheeks were frozen in motion across the expanse. Waves of soft music bounced off the image, cascading onto the crowd of finely dressed people like misty rain on a humid summer day. They held flutes of champagne and their laughter, genuine or insincere, mixed in with the echo of the music. The small quartet in the corner of the room was playing quartet Number Fourteen, in G major, by Wolfgang Amadeus Mozart.

Elizabeth watched as Beethoven crept into the room through the tall double doors encrusted with scrolls and floral decorations. He kept along the wall and watched the people mingling in the room. Elizabeth weaved herself through the mass of people, hoping to seize the opportunity to speak with the guest. However, she was two steps behind another pursuer of

Beethoven's attention. The man was round in the middle, causing the buttons of his coat to strain. The mustache under his nose was equivalent in thickness.

"My good sir," the man's voice roared. He placed a hand on Beethoven's shoulder and his mustache curled in a smile. "It is truly an honor to be in your presence. I adore your performances and I admire your perseverance to continue performing and conducting and whatnot, given your condition. It is tinnitus, is it not? What a shame. What a burden for a man of your talent to carry. Pardon me, I am gabbling, aren't I? My name is Leopold Gross."

Beethoven stared at him blankly. Realizing that the man had paused in the expectancy of a reply, he nodded and walked away. Elizabeth huffed and followed him. The weight of her velvet dress constricted her, but she managed to catch up. Placing a hand on his arm, she received his attention.

He turned around to face her, his large eyes dominating the features of his face. His lips and chin were both small and slightly pouty. His thick eyebrows rose expectantly at her stillness. She was taken aback by her own pause; so many questions and thoughts to share with him had all vanished. Hastily forming a smile, she curtsied to him and extended a gloved hand. He took it in his own hand and kissed the middle knuckles lightly. Using her other hand, Elizabeth gestured toward the dancing. Beethoven shook his head.

"I take pity on a woman who attempts to dance with me," he said bluntly.

Chapter Four

January 1809

Nicholas was sitting at his large office desk when the letter was borne into the room, perched upon its silver platter as if to royalty itself. Peeling off the waxy bind of the stamp, Nicholas unfolded the letter and skimmed the contents. He laughed with joy at the letter's message, quickly rose from his seat and exited the room.

The music coming from the piano in the sitting room filled the walls with vibrations that made the entire house appear to be humming. Elizabeth played the keys delicately; her long fingers stroked the ivory with a gentle touch. Her dark hair cascaded down in curls and brushed against her arms as she played. She continued the piece, even as she noticed out of the corner of her eye her father entering the room. She finished the piece with a dramatic chord and then turned to face the tall man with a smile.

"I believe you are improving, Elise," Nicholas said, nodding his head towards the piano. "No doubt Herr Beethoven will be impressed at your first lesson."

"He has agreed to teach me?" Elizabeth asked, her voice high pitched with excitement.

"Indeed he has. You begin next week."

"What wonderful news. I must tell Mariana." Elizabeth was leaving the room before she could finish her sentence. Dashing down the hall, Elizabeth nearly crashed into the butler who was carrying a tray with a cup of hot chocolate for Nicholas. He easily maneuvered around her, having years of practice veering out of the girl's way. Ever since she was young, Elizabeth had a spirit that lightened the mood of any distressed soul. Sliding down the wood floors in her socks, Elizabeth found Mariana in the laundry room. Mariana's eyes widened as Elizabeth entered too quickly and nearly fell down.

"My lady," Mariana cried out as she reached for Elizabeth's arms to help steady her. "You enter with such force, how do you avoid injury?"

"Practice," Elizabeth laughed. "I had to come quickly. I couldn't bear to keep the information to myself any longer."

"What is it? Is it so urgent that you must

scare me as you do?"

"Herr Beethoven has agreed to give me lessons. I begin next week."

"That is wonderful news." She smiled and wrapped her arms around Elizabeth. "I am so very proud of you, Elise. You have so much to learn from this opportunity."

Chapter Five

January 1809

The small carriage that Elizabeth was riding in bounced along the cobbled street of a busy avenue bustling with folk in the morning air. Women mingled in the market place and bargained for the best deals on chicken and goods. Wary of the horse carriages, children ran screaming though the streets, chasing one another with sword-imagined sticks.

Elizabeth glanced out the window, the wide fanned bill of her bonnet tapping along the glass window. The blue ribbon that held the hat to her head matched the periwinkle blue muslin material of her dress. Mariana sat beside her. Sensing Elizabeth's nervousness, the older woman grabbed her hand and squeezed it tenderly.

Turning off the busy street, the carriage maneuvered down a small alleyway and stopped in front of an old, two-story apartment building. Elizabeth looked up at the windows of the building, glazed with silt. The carriage driver opened the door and offered a hand.

"My lady," he said.

"This cannot be it," Elizabeth argued, her mouth open as she continued to look up. "I imagined Herr Beethoven's estate to be more of an…estate."

"I assure you, Lady Elise, we are at the correct location. We will remain outside until your lesson has finished."

"Thank you."

Elizabeth looked at Mariana, who nodded at her encouragingly. Cautiously, Elizabeth walked up to the door and knocked twice. An older woman answered after a moment. Her face was warm as she smiled.

"Hello," she said sweetly. "You must be here for a lesson. He's right upstairs. Door to the right."

"Thank you, Madame," Elizabeth answered, stepping into the building. The old woman closed the door behind them and gestured to the stairs against the wall.

"Right this way dear," the woman explained. Her messy grey hair was pulled into a bun on the back of her head and the apron she wore was stained with red jam. Elizabeth held onto the banister tightly as she wandered up the stairs. The boards creaked under her weight.

The sound of laughter reverberated from behind the closed door that the elderly woman had mentioned. Curious, Elizabeth crept up to it and slowly turned the handle. Through a space of the door, she saw Beethoven embracing a woman in a scarlet dress with ivory lace embellishments, their lips interlocked. Uneasy with what she had seen, Elizabeth backed away, and knocked on the door, louder than necessary. Seconds later, Beethoven opened the door.

"Ah, yes," he said, speaking to the other woman. "Lady Elizabeth Braun is here for her lesson. Unfortunately, I must bid you farewell, my fair visitor."

The woman sauntered over to him and extended her hand.

"It was a pleasure," he said and kissed her

hand.

She moved past Elizabeth and departed. Turning to Elizabeth, Beethoven nodded his head and extended his hand to welcome her into the room.

"It's you," Beethoven said with a smile. "The dancer."

"Yes," Elizabeth said. "I'm Elizabeth Braun. You can call me Elise if you like."

"I'm sorry, my dear, my hearing is not very sharp today. The concert this weekend took a toll on my ears. Who knew that standing closest to the orchestra would cause you to absorb the loudest sounds? If you have something to say, please write it down to show me."

He gestured to a notebook on the table, surrounded by messy stacks of paper.

Elizabeth held up her own notebook for him to see and opened it to the first page.

She wrote: 'My name is Elizabeth. You can call me Elise if you wish. It is a pleasure to meet you and I am delighted that you have agreed to give me lessons.'

"Splendid," Beethoven nodded. "Shall we begin our first lesson, Elizabeth?"

Chapter Six

February 1809

Elizabeth strode into the dining room, where Nicholas was waiting for her to begin their dinner. She had the blushful smile of someone with a scandalous secret. Although suspicious of this expression, Nicholas pushed back the urge to reprimand his daughter.

"How was your lesson, Elise?"

"It was quite wonderful." Elizabeth's voice was quick with excitement. "Herr Beethoven is a magnificent teacher. I am learning about the dynamics of music and how the volume can evoke different emotions for the listener. It is rather fascinating to know how much feeling goes into playing. The art takes the entire body and soul to create the purest sound. I feel as though I am learning so much more than just regular techniques. I am learning about the soul."

"That sounds marvelous, my dear," Nicholas said, attempting to hide the concern in his tone. Her excitement put him on edge, but he didn't want to reveal any concern. "I hope that you are not uncomfortable, learning from such an older man."

"Oh, I hardly see Herr Beethoven as an older man," Elizabeth explained with confidence. "Rather as a more experienced man."

Uneasy because of her statement, Nicholas excused himself from the table. His appetite had left him and he moved into his office.

He took a sheet of parchment from the desk drawer and sat down in the tall backed chair. Using the feather pen on the desk, Nicholas composed a short letter. His cursive letters swooped and curved with a scratch. He signed his name at the end and sealed the letter in an envelope. The butler entered the room at the ping of the small bell on the desk corner.

"Yes, sir?"

"Send this letter first thing tomorrow," Nicholas answered. "It is to Maximilian Wahs."

The butler started to leave before Nicholas spoke again.

"And will you please send Mariana in here?"

Nicholas drummed his fingers on the edge

of the desk while he waited for the tall woman to enter. She entered the room with a confident stride, holding herself in a respectful manner.

"Mariana, may I have a brief word with you?"

"Of course, sir," she replied politely.

"I am concerned with the manner in which Elizabeth speaks of Herr Beethoven. I do not want to indulge my discomfort, but I do want a woman's opinion on whether it is indeed justified."

"I believe you have nothing to worry about, my lord. I find Elizabeth's admiration to arise from the fact that she is learning from a man with such talent. While she has experience with upper class citizens, she has not met many talented musicians or artists, and she is expressing her excitement to that. I do not believe there is any more to it."

"That is relieving. I do not want to worry about the unnecessary. However, I have invited Maximilian to visit for dinner soon. I am hopeful that Elizabeth will grow fond of him soon. His father is becoming quite impatient with her lack of enthusiasm and my desire for time before their marriage."

"She will learn to."

Nicholas nodded for her to leave and Mariana's dress wrinkled as she curtsied. Nicholas sat himself in his office chair, took the feather quill out of its container, and returned his attention to the estate documents on the desk before him.

Z. D. GARNER

Chapter Seven

February 1809

"Again," Beethoven barked. He was staring out the window of the room through the thick window. The street beneath his apartment was empty; all of its passersby were at the next street over, busy at the marketplace. The early morning brought about summer heat that filtered into the small apartment room. Elizabeth played her scales and arpeggios a third time.

"How do you know?" she asked arbitrarily.

"How do I know what?" he replied, keeping his attention outside.

"How do you know if I am doing well or not? You refuse to watch me today."

"It's a funny thing, my hearing is," he explained. "Some days it is adequate, never perfect, but sufficient. Other times, it ceases to exist and I must rely on my hands to feel and my eyes to see. It's worst in large crowds. Not a single soul knows how to refrain from shouting. Today, my ears are well, so I am not required to watch you play something as elementary as scales. One last time before we get to the sonata, if you please."

She nodded even though he was not looking at her and began the task once more. Out of the corner of her vision, she watched him. He tapped his foot impatiently and continued to stare intensely out of the window.

A knock at the door interrupted her playing. Beethoven answered it swiftly, and without speaking more than three words to the gentleman, returned to the window with a letter in hand. He read the letter briefly, crumpled the piece of paper up, and threw it aside with a growl.

"What is the matter?" Elizabeth asked cautiously.

"They shorted me again, those slimy rats," he hissed, and smacked a handful of coins on the table. "They think I won't notice these things but I do. I always do. And they always pay me less than promised. I knew it. I knew they would. Those bastards."

A stack of papers and the coins were sent flying by the sweep of his arm across the table. Elizabeth flinched and watched him return to the window, his fists curled and his knuckles white.

"Why not confront them?" Elizabeth asked, carefully rising from the piano bench.

"Oh, believe me," Beethoven snarled. "I will."

Elizabeth approached him, but her heel caught on a split in the wood floor. She stumbled and it caught Beethoven's attention. He looked at her with a raised eyebrow.

"I need a moment," he murmured. The piano bench made an abrupt scraping sound as he positioned himself. With a quick breath, he began his piece and his fingers bounced off the keys with each aggressive chord. When he finished, his hands trembled in his lap and there was a silence hanging in the air.

"You are so very – " Elizabeth began before he cut her off.

"Don't say it," he growled. "I know what you are going to say, but don't."

"What?"

"Boorish, explosive, barbaric. You were going to say something along those lines, but don't."

"I was going to say," Elizabeth began again. "Passionate."

Beethoven glanced at her, his breathing audible. He was shocked by the kindness and admiration in her blue eyes. Shaking his head, he moved towards her and placed a stack of music on the stand in front of her.

"Show me what you have practiced," he instructed. "We need to find you an opportunity to perform soon."

Elizabeth smiled and took her place back on the piano bench.

Chapter Eight

February 1809

"Johann Schneider?" Claudia's mouth hung open as she gaped at her friend, Maria. "*The* Johann Schneider?"

"The very one," Maria answered with a cocked eyebrow. Her deep brown hair was tied at the nape of her neck. A few stranded curls framed around her face.

"I cannot believe you are already engaged to be married," Elizabeth said, sipping from her cup. "It seems as though just yesterday we were playing with dolls and braving the outdoors together."

"I resent that," Claudia said with a still expression. Her natural rosy cheeks stood out against her milk-white skin and fair hair.

"Why?" Elizabeth asked.

"I still play with dolls," Claudia replied before bursting into a fit of laughter. The other two joined in the chorus of giggles that echoed around the tall sitting room. Dressed in light fabric dresses, the women were at Claudia's estate to have brunch together.

"Even if we did play with dolls yesterday," Maria began. "I am not too young to be getting married. Neither are you, Elise. How soon do you suppose you will be married to Maximilian?"

"Not likely," Elizabeth said, scrunching her nose in distaste. "I am much too busy focusing on my piano lessons."

"You are taking lessons with Herr Beethoven, are you not?" Claudia asked, her face alight with interest. "He is quite magnificent at the piano. Have you learned much?"

"I am not splendid at the piano, but he has been quite patient with me."

Maria scoffed.

"I'm surprised," she huffed. "But I have heard that he is more careful of his temper around beautiful women."

"Does he ever walk around in his underwear?" Claudia asked curiously. "I heard he composes in his underwear or naked. Even when he has company over."

"I hear he hardly bathes," Maria laughed. "Can you imagine being around someone so filthy?"

"It's because he is so dedicated to his work," Elizabeth explained. "He believes that he shouldn't waste a moment, lest the melody flee from his head."

"For a man of such dedication, he is lacking in the personal hygiene department."

"As well as proper etiquette," Claudia added. "Did you know that he shouts at anyone that talks during his performance?"

"He's such a boorish man," Maria said. "Doesn't he know how to express any other emotion than anger?"

"Quite so," Elizabeth cut in. "It's all in his music. Love, beauty, anger, fear. It's all there. He has mastered transposing feelings into sound that strikes the most human-like nerves in our bodies. Hearing his music is identical to having a conversation with him. He tells you more about the intimacy of life and nature than you could ever know."

"Music about love doesn't make the man worthy of it."

"In my opinion, he is a fine man," Elizabeth argued. "He is more than capable of a successful marriage."

"I pray you do not mean with yourself."

Maria glanced half-worriedly half-unbelievingly at Claudia. Elizabeth remained silent.

"You must understand, Elise," Maria began. "Marriage is about status. Your status is valuable. So much so, that you must protect its authenticity. Valuable status can only be shared with other valuable status if it is to remain valuable. The status of the élite must be upheld so, or else we would die out."

"But what about love," Elizabeth argued. "I can't imagine that status is more important than that."

"Love doesn't matter. You can grow to love anyone, that's why arranged marriages develop into actual romances over time. You can fall in love with anyone under the right circumstances."

"Is this what I have to look forward to with Maximilian Wahs?" Elizabeth sighed, sitting back in her chair with crossed arms.

"You should consider yourself fortunate that you caught the eye of such a successful man, Elise," Claudia said, touching her friend's arm. "He is courageous and kind."

"Not to mention handsome," Maria added.

"He is not passionate."

"He may not have Herr Beethoven's vigor, but Maximilian has something more," Claudia continued. "He is caring and he will serve you well as a husband. You shall never want from him."

"Claudia is right. Herr Beethoven is a selfish man, Elise," Maria said, her tone firm. "And selfish people live lonely lives."

Elizabeth nodded, trying to avoid having the conversation go any more in a direction she didn't want it to. The rest of the afternoon she was quiet, only listening to the opinions that her two friends had to offer.

Chapter Nine

March 1809

The tall room of the estate was lit up in a glow from the light of the dozens of candelabras that lined the walls. The smell of cake and champagne drifted through the air, exciting the nostrils of those who whiffed the scent. Elizabeth lifted her skirt as she walked to avoid dragging the delicate fabric across the floor. She approached Maria and wrapped her in an embrace.

"Maria, darling," she said, sweetly. "You look absolutely stunning tonight with that new piece of jewelry on your finger."

"It is quite a treasure," Maria replied, holding her engagement ring in the light so it gleamed magnificently.

Taking her hand, Elizabeth ran her eyes over the gold details of the ring and smiled.

"Exquisite."

Elizabeth craned her neck to see the man behind Maria. His arm was slipped around Maria's waist and he wore an Austrian uniform.

"You are a fortunate man, Johann," she said teasingly. "Or should I call you Corporal Schneider?"

"Indeed I am, Elise," the man answered with a cocked eyebrow. He looked at Maria, hardly able to hide his pride in his smile. "Maria is the most beautiful in all of Vienna."

"Only when she is having a ball thrown in her honor," Claudia inserted herself into the conversation. Maria scoffed at the jest, but laughed it off with the rest of the group. The quartet began a new piece, a lively waltz that filled the room.

"Shall we, my dear?" Johann said, extending a hand to his fiancé. The couple exited the circle and began moving across the center of the room. Their movements were fluid and they seemed to move as one person, rather than two.

Elizabeth was watching them so intensely that she did not hear someone approach behind her. An unexpected hand on her shoulder briefly scared her and she turned her head quickly. Maximilian stood tall directly behind her, and he smiled down at her. The blue of his eyes was enhanced by the white shirt and blue scarf he wore.

"Elise," he said without his smile fading, "how lovely to see you again. This is quite the engagement ball, wouldn't you agree?"

"I suppose so," Elizabeth said lightly. She could feel the muscles in her body tensing up. The hand remaining on her shoulder did not help. "It is very extravagant, but that is how Maria is."

"That is a valid point."

The pair was quiet for a moment. At the same time, they both tried to speak.

"You first," Maximilian said politely.

"No, you," Elizabeth contradicted. "I insist."

"Very well. Would you care to dance?"

Despite her lack of interest, Elizabeth knew that denying him would result in a painfully long conversation with her father later. She could almost feel his eyes burning into her with an intense stare.

"It would be a pleasure," Elizabeth said, trying to keep the sarcasm creeping onto her tongue at bay.

~~~

When the dance ended, the party was escorted into the room adjacent to the ballroom. The audience was seated in a large semi circle around the piano. The grand was a deep shade of brown, and every inch of it glossed to shine in even the dimmest of lighting. The keys of the piano, seamlessly aligned and shaped in perfect symmetry to each other, stretched their black and white pattern across the front of the instrument.

Maria and Johann were sitting together in the front and middle of the audience. Elizabeth was next to Maria and Claudia sat on the other side. Elizabeth's gloved hands gripped the arms of her chair as she anticipated the performance.

Beethoven was escorted into the room by the butler, who held the door open for the performer to enter. Nodding his head at the audience, Beethoven sat splay-legged on the bench and hovered his hands over the keys. With the first chord, Elizabeth let out a breath that she had not realized she had been holding. The low minor chords in the bass were suspended in the air like a mist above the continuous melody that drove the piece in a slow moving progression.

A low conversation was being held to the right of Elizabeth and she looked to see two gentlemen having a quiet conversation. Although the conversation was not overly loud to bother the guests, Elizabeth was furious at their lack of focus on the performance. She wondered if their rude gesture was aimed at the fact that Beethoven could not hear them whisper.

Despite their attempt to keep quiet, Beethoven saw the movement of the conversation out of the corner of his eye. Suddenly, he stopped playing and placed his hands on his legs. Tilting his body slightly, he stared at the gentlemen. The focus and coldness in his eyes could have made them turn into the two spheres of ice that were in his head. The unblinking stare continued even after the gentlemen had returned his gaze and ceased to speak. A dead silence hung in the air as he continued to look at them.

Then he returned to playing, right where he had left off. As if nothing had happened.

Z. D. GARNER

Chapter Ten

March 1809

"Did you ever meet Mozart?" Elizabeth inquired. Her skirt twisted as she turned on the piano bench to face Ludwig. Her hands were held together on her lap and she looked at him expectantly. Her eyes appeared larger with her hair pulled back into a tight bun at the crown of her head.

"Which one do you speak of?" Ludwig looked at her and then quickly away, embarrassed to stare too long. "Wolfgang, or his father Leopold?"

"Wolfgang."

"I did," he answered, walking to the window to look out. "It was brief. I had traveled here to Vienna to perform for him, hoping that he would take me on as a student. It was planned for me to begin lessons with him, but alas, with the events of my family followed by his death a few years later, I was never able to."

"What did he say to you when you performed for him?"

"Nothing to me. Yet, I found out later what he had said in regards to me."

"What was that?"

"He said, 'Keep your eyes on him. Someday he'll give the world something to talk about'."

"That's wonderful." Elizabeth smiled.

"It's wrong. He is wrong. Do you know how many things I could have learned from him? How much better I could be?" Ludwig spat and his hands clenched into tight fists. "I could actually have been successful in composing operas, the most accomplished work that a musician can write. The world won't talk about me. They barely do now."

"That's not true," Elizabeth argued, her voice gentle. "You are the most talented pianist in all of Vienna."

"I could be better," Ludwig yelled. He slammed his arms on the desk near the window and sent a scatter of parchment flying around the room. Heavy breathing caused the back of his coat to stretch as his chest expanded. The papers made light sounds as they reached the floor. Elizabeth stood up and approached Ludwig cautiously, placing her hands on his back and arm.

"Your music," she began softly, her fingers tenderly squeezing the fabric of his clothes. "It affects more people than you know. In ways that you can't possibly imagine. You affect the soul of a person. Your music, it makes people human."

Elizabeth stooped down to begin retrieving the array of papers across the floor. As she organized the loose papers into piles, she came across an unopened letter.

"This letter," she said curiously. "It is dated almost ten years ago. You never opened it?"

"I am aware. It is from my brother. I already know what it says."

"How could you possibly know?"

"Because of the letter I sent him first. He is reassuring me of his love and advising me against taking my life."

"You were planning on taking your life?" Elizabeth asked, aghast. Her eyes were wide.

"When my hearing first began to fail, I ceased to see a reason to live. Music is so important to me, I could not bear to live without it. In the end, I decided that I had too much left to compose."

"The world is grateful for that," Elizabeth said. "And so am I."

Ludwig looked up from the desk, his eyes gleamed around the brim with wetness. Reaching for Elizabeth's hand, he pulled her into a tight hug.

"A harsh man such as I does not deserve the compassion that you have given," he said near her ear. "And for that I am thankful."

Elizabeth pulled tighter on her arms

around his back before she moved away. Looking up at him, her cheeks grew pink as she thought of a question to ask.

"I know this is none of my business, but I must admit I am quite curious," she began. "The woman who was here just before my first lesson. Who is she?"

"That was quite some time ago," Ludwig looked away as he thought. "Ah yes, that must have been Lady Rosaline Mussini. I met her at a ball about a year ago. Her husband had asked me to perform at their estate for the evening. Rude man, he had no respect for my playing. Rosaline did, however, and she was determined to let me know of her admirations in her own way during her visits to my apartment."

"She is married?"

"Quite so. She is convinced that it is

unhappily and by being so it gives her the excuse to fulfill her happiness elsewhere."

"That is outrageous. An élite woman sneaking about under her own rules of reason."

"She is very strong-headed, but I suppose that is why we got along so well," Ludwig laughed, ignoring the disgusted expression that Elizabeth wore. "I haven't seen her lately. She and her husband moved to England recently."

"That is good to hear. I am not very fond of competition."

"Competition?" Ludwig asked. Without warning, Elizabeth leaned him into the wall behind him and pressed her lips to his. Despite the surprise, he didn't stop her.

Chapter Eleven

April 1809

"Good morning, Elizabeth," Maximilian said with a smile. He was sitting at the breakfast table next to Nicholas. They both looked at her as she entered the room.

"Good morning, father," she said tentatively. "And Maximilian."

"Max is enough," Maximilian replied.

"I know it comes as a pleasant surprise, Elise," Nicholas began.

"It certainly is a surprise," Elizabeth said

with a tight smile, swiping her napkin off the table and placing it in her lap.

"I have invited Max to spend the afternoon with you."

Elizabeth responded with silence and began eating her breakfast.

"I was hoping we could go into town and look at some of the new shops that recently opened. Then have lunch in the salon and return here for a pleasant stroll through the grounds."

Elizabeth nodded. At least she would have plenty distractions to hold her attention.

~~~

After breakfast, the pair climbed into a carriage drawn up in the driveway of the estate. Elizabeth wore a light green dress and matching bonnet. Maximilian was sitting far closer than she wanted him to be, but there was little to do about it in the small carriage. Once they had left the sight of the estate, and the sight of Nicholas, Maximilian moved even closer to Elizabeth.

"What are you doing?" she questioned as she leaned away.

"I was hoping you would let me steal a kiss."

"I do have some decency."

"That's not true."

"What do you mean?" Elizabeth asked, facing the window but keeping him warily in sight.

"You kissed me when we were younger."

"We were children. That means nothing."

"And I'm sure you have kissed others,

maybe even this Herr Beethoven your father thinks you are so fond of."

Elizabeth held her composure, but she could feel heat flow to her cheeks. She hoped it wasn't noticeable.

"It seems you think of me as a young girl and not as I am now, a lady."

"Of course not," he answered. He dropped the conversation and looked out the opposite window. Elizabeth exhaled, realizing she had been holding her breath.

~~~

"This is quite a lovely dress," Maximilian said, gesturing to a gown in the store shop window in front of him.

"I am not fond of it."

"Why not? The detail is very intricate."

"The color is not ideal to me."

The dress hanging in the window was a long white gown with extravagant pearl and lace detail. Elizabeth moved on from the shop and entered the bookstore next door. Maximilian followed her and watched her movements as she stroked her hand along the spines of the rows of books.

"I was unaware you were a reader," he said in a hushed voice.

"I am not really," Elizabeth explained. "But I do enjoy the display of a full library. It has so many options, so many endless possibilities waiting behind the hard spine. No one ever tells you which book you need to read or which you should not. It's freedom."

"I myself am not a reader either," Maximilian began. He droned on for several minutes, to the point where Elizabeth stopped listening.

Chapter Twelve

April 1809

"One would deem the paintings on the inner walls of their estate to be beautiful, but alas, it is a mere imitation of the spectacle that lies, open in the real thing," Elizabeth said.

The fabric of her pale blue dress was light and floated around her at even the hint of a breeze. The dirt trail had a layer of dust that kicked up a few inches off the ground. The morning sun tinted the sky the color of a robin's breast, a rich flush that seemed to Elizabeth frozen in time.

"Indeed," Ludwig responded, breathing in the air deeply. Ludwig had paced the trail a hundred times over, each time springing a new inspiration. He would stroll through, what he thought, was the atmosphere of God.

On this particular day, he had asked Elizabeth to join him.

"The experience can only truly be had in the presence of nature, not simply in that of the imitation," he explained.

The pair walked in peaceful silence, allowing only the sound of their footsteps to interrupt the melody of the landscape. Every few moments, Elizabeth would glance at the man beside her. His dark eyebrows were furrowed in the center over his large eyes, which were focused on the environment around. The skin on his face was worn from exposure to sun and wind. His posture was angled downward slightly so that his eyes focused on the ground a few feet ahead. Arms behind his back, he seemed to be a man who was pacing, rather than walking.

Elizabeth touched his arm, gently enough to catch his attention. He stopped mid-stride and turned his body to face her, a curious expression pulling his eyebrows upward. She took his arms and placed one on her hip. She clasped the other between her fingers.

Realizing her intentions, Ludwig began to pull away. Elizabeth held tight to his hand, and placed both of her palms around it, holding it close to her chest. Her eyes pleaded, seeming almost desperate. He hesitated, trying to avoid fear from showing on his face. She noticed it though, seeing the brief flash of uncertainty that his eyes revealed. His gaze was turned away, but his eyes failed him when he looked back at her. Fighting with his own self-consciousness, he gave in to her plea, replacing his arm on her side. His grip was strong and Elizabeth could sense his nervousness through the grasp of his fingers. Pushing up on her toes, Elizabeth leaned toward his ear.

"Simple three-step waltz. I'll lead."

Moving back, she met his eyes and smiled, hoping to ease his uncertainty. She mouthed the beats, counting them in and bouncing to get the rhythm matched between them. Twice through and she began to dance, pulling him along with her as they shifted. Ludwig's back was stiff as she moved him around. Becoming accustomed to the pattern of the dance, he became more relaxed.

Instinctively, his arms brought her closer to him and he took over. Elizabeth laughed as she felt the change and looked up at him. He was smiling. Great teeth exposed by tight lips that stretched wide and pushed his cheek muscles up so that his eyes became crescent shaped. He had never smiled at Elizabeth before. Her heart fluttered and forced hot blood into her cheeks. Distracted and embarrassed, Elizabeth lost her footing and stumbled. Catching her in a pseudo-dip, Ludwig laughed and held her gaze. Recognizing the pause far later than he should, he pulled her back upright, noticing her hold on his arms.

Elizabeth pulled away from him, her hands distracted by the fabric of her dress. The pair stood in awkward hesitation before, without warning, Ludwig pulled out a small notebook from his jacket and scribbled down something that Elizabeth could not see. He hummed as he did so. Before Elizabeth could ask what he was writing, the notebook was slid back into his jacket pocket and Ludwig gestured for them to continue their walk.

"Shall we?" he invited, softly.

As the pair continued to walk, the silence between them was maintained. Not out of a lack of conversation, but admiration for the natural world around them in the pleasure of one another's company as they walked.

Chapter Thirteen

April 1809

"What will he do next?" Leopold Gross said with a booming voice. "Take over Russia?"

"He managed to take over France," the old woman with gray hair argued. "You can never be sure of his intentions."

"Oh, yes, Lady Margaret. France was such a challenge," Gross responded with a laugh.

"Regardless, the Emperor of France," Nicholas began. Booing sounds and hisses from around the room interrupted him. He raised his voice to be heard. "Whether or not we call him an Emperor, he is the official one of France. Can we please focus?"

"Nicholas is right," Lady Margaret sighed. "What are we going to do about the on coming army?"

"We defeated him before and we can do it again," Gross shouted. "Our troops are more than capable."

"His army has been growing," Nicholas countered. "Are we willing to take that risk? Our families could be at stake."

The salon filled with low mumbles as the group talked amongst themselves.

"What do you propose we do, Nicholas?" Lady Margaret asked.

"I, myself, am considering that Elizabeth

and I will go visit my parents in Hamburg," Nicholas explained. He put a hand on his jaw as he thought. "It is the only way I can assure her safety."

"Are you suggesting that we all run away?" Gross spat. "Like cowards? Dogs with our tail between our legs?"

"What I am suggesting," Nicholas growled back, "is that you consider your lives and the lives of your wife and children, above your own overweening pride."

Chapter Fourteen

May 1809

Elizabeth was returning home from having lunch with Maria and Claudia, when she noticed the immense bustle happening at her front door. Through the thin window of the carriage, she could see a multitude of servants in dark uniform loading up wagon after wagon with cases and items from the estate. Eyebrows furrowed in concern, Elizabeth leaped from the carriage and approached the butler overlooking the affair.

"What in God's name is happening?"

Distaste and confusion rang in her voice. "Surely, we are not being evicted."

"Certainly not, my lady," the butler answered. "Recent news has informed your family that Napoleon and his French troops are on their way to Vienna. I imagine you are aware of how the French feel about the élite. Your father has called for an immediate trip to visit your family in Germany."

"Where is Papa? I must speak with him."

"He is in his office," the butler's voice grew louder to reach the departing girl. "Mind his temper, the stress of the situation has him on edge."

Elizabeth's feet made padding sounds as she crossed the floor to the office. Noticing the two shut doors, she knocked to introduce her presence.

"Enter," the stern voice of her father spoke from behind the wood. Pushing the heavy door open, Elizabeth entered the room. Her father was facing the window, a hand to his chin as he inspected the activity in the driveway below. His expression changed when he turned and recognized his daughter standing in the entrance. "Ah, Elise, I see you have finally arrived. I apologize for the shock of the sudden change. I received a letter from General Wahs an hour ago alerting us of Napoleon's troops. They will be in Vienna in a few days. We must leave for Germany at once."

"Leave? Papa, I don't understand why we must leave. We are not involved in the affairs of government. Surely, we will not be reckoned with."

"I will not risk the lives of my family in the face of war. It is too dangerous to stay and take that chance."

Elizabeth nodded and looked down.

"How long do you expect we will be gone?" she asked, her lips pinched together in anticipation of a hopeful answer.

"I cannot be sure, but I would guess a few months." Noticing her reaction, Nicholas raised his voice. "Judging from the previous lengths of the battles. I am hoping that it will be less than that."

"Several months?" Elizabeth's face reflected the dislike in her voice. "That sounds absolutely dreadful."

"Unfortunately, we do not have the luxury of time to discuss the matter any further. Please go prepare yourself for our journey, Elise."

Chapter Fifteen

May 1809

A cannon fired, sending gunpowder spewing and an iron ball smashed through the wall of a nearby building. The sounds echoed down the streets and the firing of guns seemed minuscule in comparison. Ludwig was in a pile on the floor in the middle of the room with his brother and sister in law. He covered his head with his arms, squeezing his forearms against his ears in an attempt to protect his hearing.

~~~

Hundreds of miles away, Elizabeth, safely

ensconced on her grandmother's estate in Germany, stared out a tall window, passing the time before the upcoming performance in the piano room. Her thin fingers were shaking with the nervousness that gripped her whole body.

~~~

Dirt rose up from the solid ground, sticking to the sweat on Ludwig's face. Desperate to preserve his ears, he pressed his arms tighter against them until he could feel the pulsing of the blood in his head. With each loud explosion, a continuous ringing erupted from his eardrums.

~~~

Elizabeth positioned herself on the piano bench, adjusting herself to find the perfect spot. She smiled at the audience, a small crowd, consisting of her grandmother and father as well as her grandmother's friends. Her hands floated above the keys and pressed down gently on the first notes. Her touch was light and delicate. Ludwig hated the way she played his piece. He thought she played without feeling. But she did so when she thought of him.

~~~

His level of vulnerability left Ludwig trembling. Bullets screamed through the air. The overwhelming sounds of battle sought to control him, demanding his attention and submission, like the father that beat him. He saw, in the surrounding violence, his father drunk and angry. The shaking of the entire room reminded him of being thrown to the floor, unable to wake up and move his body at three in the morning in order to practice. Struggling to play the correct notes in the correct order. Always ending with his father's crashing fist.

~~~

Elizabeth continued to play. The bittersweet chords of the Moonlight Sonata seemed suspended in the space above, filling the entirety of the tall room. Gray light seeped through the windows and filled the air with a musty glow like a thin veil. The small taps of raindrops hit the glass of the windows.

~~~

Ludwig lay on his side; the cold embrace of the ground comforted him. Tears lined with dirt slid down his face. The empty basement shook and he could feel the vibrations shaking his body, even though the whole world had gone terribly silent.

ELISE

Part Two

After the Invasion

Chapter Sixteen

April 1810

"Are you nervous, dear?" Mariana asked Elizabeth. They were sitting in a carriage outside Beethoven's new apartment. Mariana placed her hand on top of Elizabeth's to stop her from fidgeting with her handkerchief. Elizabeth looked at the woman, her blue eyes wide.

"Not quite," Elizabeth explained. "I have a strange feeling. I am not sure what caused this."

"Do not fret, Elise," Mariana said with

softness. "It is likely nothing. You worry over nothing."

Elizabeth nodded curtly and exited the carriage. Hesitation pulled at her every movement. A small section of her dress was crumpled from the tightness of her grip on the fabric. Without knocking, Elizabeth entered the apartment.

The second time that Elizabeth interrupted Ludwig in the company of a woman, was more of a shock than the first, despite the difference in situation. The woman was young; her long hair was tied up in a knot under the elaborate hat she wore. The ribbons that decorated the hat matched the fabric of the dress she wore in both pattern and shine.

"My apologies," Elizabeth stammered, beginning to exit as quickly as she had entered. "I did not realize you were with company."

"No, stay, Elizabeth," Ludwig insisted. "We are nearly finished here."

He turned his attention to the woman in front of him again. She was tall and lean, with a confident disposition that caused her elegant body to tower over Elizabeth.

"I would appreciate it greatly if you were to look over this and give me your thoughts," he said to the woman. "This piece is new and means a great deal to me."

"I shall cherish it, as if it were dedicated to myself," the woman answered, her voice quiet. She kissed Ludwig on both cheeks, nodded to Elizabeth and departed the room.

"Who was that woman?" Elizabeth asked immediately. Having anticipated that she would speak, Ludwig gestured to his ears and pointed at the notebook Elizabeth held in her left hand.

"Of course," Elizabeth whispered. She felt guilty for constantly forgetting that his hearing had deteriorated further. She was very upset when she had first learned about it upon returning from Germany, only a month after French troops had appeased Vienna.

Elizabeth turned to a blank page and scribbled down her words. She showed him after she had completed her question.

"Her name," he replied, "is Therese Malfatti. She is a new student and I have become acquainted with her family over the past month. She is a very kind and mature woman."

A hot shock of electric heat ran over Elizabeth's body, causing the hair to stand on end in an uncomfortable manner. She tried to hide her jealousy by smiling, but the tightness of her lips gave her away. Ludwig noticed this.

"You need not worry about Miss Malfatti, Elizabeth," he said, taking both her hands. "Now, onto why I asked you to meet me here today."

His sudden pause frightened and excited her at the same time. She anticipated his next words.

"Elizabeth, I would like for you to play a duet with me at the upcoming ball hosted by the Malfatti family."

Stunned by the offer, Elizabeth shook away her misperception and nodded her head. An excited smile grew on Ludwig's face.

"Excellent. Now, in order to be ready in time, I would like to increase your lessons to three per week. Would your father agree to this?"

Elizabeth thought for a moment. Their

lessons had taken place at her estate since her return, due to Ludwig's removing the legs of the pianos in his apartment. Her father had seemed to enjoy the music that echoed throughout the house. Elizabeth nodded at Ludwig's question.

"Wonderful," he said.

Chapter Seventeen

May 1810

"No, no," Ludwig said gruffly. "Like this."

He played a section of the piece, his hands lifting on the off beats so that he could put more force into the down beats.

"You must learn to play with more enthusiasm. Make the piano surrender to you."

Elizabeth bobbed her head and imitated the way he had played the part. Her hands were light and delicate as they pushed on the keys. Ludwig took her hands, curling her fingers with his. He pressed down both of their hands onto the keys. The chord erupted in an enormous wave through the room.

"Try again."

Putting more weight into her fingers, Elizabeth played the section as requested.

"Splendid. Now, onto the next section."

Nicholas watched the lesson through the open door to the hall. The piano room held the sound so well that the music did not escape more widely into the estate. He found it interesting the way that Beethoven taught lessons.

Why must he sit so close on the bench?

Mariana noticed him observe.

"They do play so wonderfully together,"

she said. "Would you not agree?"

"Indeed," he replied bluntly.

"He really does bring out something in her. I have never seen her so invested in the art as now."

Nicholas nodded and continued to watch the lesson. Mariana continued.

"Her playing has improved drastically. I believe it is increasing her confidence as well."

"Mariana," Nicholas said abruptly. "Can you please get me a glass of water?"

The woman moved away with a resistant shuffle.

Nicholas observed Beethoven as he put his hands over Elizabeth's and pressed them onto the keys. With his hand on his chin, Nicholas thought to himself, aggravating his uneasiness: *Is it necessary he move her hands with his? Why can he not simply speak his mind?*

The growing anxiety in his mind became unbearable and Nicholas left the hallway to go outside.

Maybe some fresh air would clear away his suspicion. As he headed outside into the humid air, he noticed that he was humming the tune from the piano room.

"Damn it," he swore, and tried to stop.

Chapter

Eighteen

June 1810

The dining table was set at one end of the table. Cloth napkins and gleaming silver utensils were placed just so next to the glossy china. Entering the room, the two members of the Braun family were dressed in formal wear. Elizabeth thanked the butler as he pulled the chair out for her. She adjusted herself on the cushioned seat, finding a comfortable position that did not cause the tight fabric around her torso to constrict too firmly.

"Papa," Elizabeth said with a warm smile. She pulled at the ends of her cream colored gloves so that the fingers were snug. "Ludwig has asked me to perform a duet with him at the coming dinner party at the Malfatti estate. I am most excited to show what I've been practicing."

"A duet, you say?" Nicholas asked with a raised eyebrow. "That is an intimate state of playing. Are you sure that it is appropriate?"

"Quite so. Ludwig and I – "

"Elise, you know it is not proper to refer to a gentleman by his first name," he interrupted. "It is vulgar for a lady of your status."

"But, that is his name."

"Herr Beethoven is also his name," Nicholas argued. "And that is what he is to be called in this household. Furthermore, I do not want you performing a duet with him. It is not proper for a lady. Especially one of your age."

"But Papa, I have been practicing the Mozart four-hands Sonata for weeks now."

"That does not excuse the indecency of the matter."

"Ludwig has wanted to display my talents. He won't be happy to hear this."

"I am sure he will not," Nicholas laughed. "Such a hot-headed man. What doesn't make him cross?"

"He is not hot-headed," Elizabeth argued, her voice raised in anger. Her napkin and silverware fell to the floor as she stood. "He is passionate about his music and he cares about me more than you ever will."

"My office," Nicholas said after a moment. "Now."

~~~

Nicholas stormed into the office, the wide swung door smacking against the wall.

"Elise, how could you be so childish?" he demanded. He leaned his hands on the desk. Books lined the tall walls on dozens of bookshelf rows. "Yelling at the dinner table; it is unacceptable. You need to learn to act like a lady, or Maximilian will lose interest in you. We are so close to bringing the Braun and Wahs families together. I can't have you destroying the path to this union."

"I do not care for Maximilian," Elizabeth answered. "He is a pig."

Pausing a moment to compose himself, Nicholas continued.

"Elise, he worships the ground you walk on. You would be more than lucky to marry a man who cherishes you. It is rare."

"I do not love him."

"You will grow to love him. In time."

"I do not need time. I can never love him."

"He is suitable in every aspect. He is respectable, his family's image is supreme, and he is experienced in the ways of the world. What more could you possibly want from a man?"

"I want passion."

"Elizabeth, you are a lady of the élite. There are certain duties that are required of you. You cannot have everything you want."

"I want Ludwig."

The room was silent as the words hung in the air like a rotting stench. Nicholas sighed and brought a hand to his chin.

"Perhaps time is what we need to get you straightened out," he murmured to himself.

"What are you saying?"

"As soon as possible, we shall leave for Germany, where you shall become more acquainted with Maximilian and leave this fantasy behind you."

"But Papa."

"Goodnight, Elizabeth."

Elizabeth left the room, tears burning the skin on her cheeks. She entered her room to find Mariana waiting there.

"Oh, my poor Elise," she said, wrapping Elizabeth in an embrace. "The world is so cruel."

"I love him," Elizabeth stammered between gasps. "Why is that so wrong? Why can't Papa see?"

"He can. And that is why he is so worried. Your father knows more about love than he lets on," Mariana explained. "He was once extraordinarily in love."

"Do you mean with my mother?"

"Your father was not in love with your mother at first. He was madly in love with someone else, but she was not of a high enough social status. He allowed his duty and status to rule above all else. He chose your mother and learned to love her. After her death, he never moved on."

"Then why is he so harsh? Should he not understand my pain?"

"I think it is that he understands too well, Elise," Mariana said, wiping a tear from Elizabeth's chin. She felt tears in her own eyes threatening to spill over.

"I am unsure what to do."

"You don't need to know," Mariana said softly. "You just need to trust that everything will work out the way that it is meant to."

"I don't know if I can take that chance."

"You can," Mariana explained as she rose from the bed. "And you will. Now, you must rest. No more tears."

~~~

"Is she alright?" Nicholas wanted to know in a low voice. Mariana approached him from the end of the hall.

"She will be. In time."

"I cannot bear to see her this way." Nicholas shook his head and pressed his hands to his face.

"This is what's right for her. You and I

both know this."

"I know you speak the truth, but I cannot help feeling like I am doing her a wrong in keeping her from what she wants."

"Do not punish yourself for your decisions," Mariana said, reaching for Nicholas' arm. "That is in the past. Elise, she is here now. And you know what is best for her."

"That is all I want."

Nicholas looked at Mariana and smiled, his eyes still filled with sadness. He took her hand with his and moved it off his arm before walking down the hallway to his room.

Z. D. GARNER

Chapter Nineteen

June 1810

Late in the evening, Elizabeth took a carriage into town. The handkerchief that was in her hand was damp with the tears that ran down her cheeks. She could only imagine the disgusting look of her face with her trembling lips, red nose, and puffy eyes.

The carriage pulled up to the apartment and Elizabeth thanked the driver as she got out. He nodded at her. The stairs leading up to the apartment took longer to climb with the leaded feeling that Elizabeth had in her feet. She hated goodbyes.

Elizabeth had to knock a few times before the door to the apartment was opened. Ludwig was there in a plain white shirt with an assortment of stains, seeming to have just risen out of bed. His hair was even more disheveled than usual, much to Elizabeth's surprise. His eyebrows were raised at the sight of her, a mix of surprise and concern at her tears.

"Elizabeth?" he whispered. "Heavens, what is the matter?"

The words wouldn't come out of her mouth. The tears came more intensely and he invited her inside.

Ludwig sat her down and handed her a fresh handkerchief. He looked at her with concern and waited for her to write. She sniffled and tried to calm herself to the point where she could.

"I am leaving again," She wrote in the journal on her lap.

Silence hung in the air over their heads.

"How soon?" Ludwig asked, his voice was gruff as he tried to conceal his distress.

"I am unsure," Elizabeth answered, wiping her nose gently with the cloth. "Very soon I imagine. My father is not happy here and he wants to return to Germany once more."

"I don't understand. Why is he unhappy?"

"He does not like how fond I am of you."

Her forward statement shocked Ludwig. He opened his mouth to speak, but closed it. His eyes squished together as he thought.

"I am sorry," Elizabeth wrote.

"I do not blame you for decisions out of your control."

"But it is my fault. I upset him."

"Listen to me," Ludwig said, grasping her hands tightly. "You should not be expected to control your emotions. It is not human. And anyone who tells you otherwise is an incompetent fool."

Elizabeth looked at him. His large brown eyes drew her in. Embarrassed, she pulled herself away and wrote down in her notebook.

"What about the duet?"

"Perhaps we can postpone it for your return," Ludwig answered. "It would not be such a task to wait for you."

Elizabeth smiled a wobbly smile. She could feel the tears coming back. She looked away to try and hide her face, but Ludwig pulled her back with his hand.

"I have something to show you," he said with uncertainty, as if he himself did not expect what he had said. He led her over to the piano. She sat on the floor, pushing away papers scattered about to make room for herself.

Shuffling through a stack in the top drawer of his desk, Ludwig pulled out an envelope. He gently removed the papers from inside and brought them to the piano stand.

Sitting beside her, he smiled before turning his eyes to the page. His fingers floated over the white and black teeth of the instrument.

"Do you remember that day we walked in the park?" Ludwig asked her. "And you insisted that we danced?"

Elizabeth nodded her head and looked at

the lines of music.

"Well, as we did," he continued, "I heard this melody in my head. Such a light and simple melody, but so painstakingly beautiful I had to write it down."

Ludwig began to play the piece, his fingers lightly stroking the keys of the piano with upmost delicacy. The melody was smooth and light: sweet despite its minor tone.

"I composed this song in dedication to you," he said while continuing to play. "It reminds me of how you taught me to lose myself in the beauty of dance; the other side of music that I never thought myself capable of appreciating. Yet, with you, it's possible for me."

The second section of the song picked up and Ludwig smiled as he played it, almost laughing as he did. He looked so charismatic, as if he enjoyed playing in this moment more than he ever had before.

"That day in the park was when I realized that I was in love with you."

As he finished the piece, his eyes grew sentimental. Elizabeth's expression was a mixture of surprise and happiness.

"I may not know when you will return," Ludwig said, taking Elizabeth's hands. "But I will wait for you, no matter how long it may take."

"It could be years," Elizabeth wrote, her shaky hand swirling her letters messily.

"It is worth it. You are worth it. And to prove it, I will never play this song again until you return."

"You should not make that promise," Elizabeth argued. "I might not ever be able to come back. My duty to my family name insists that I marry Maximilian. I would not be happy knowing that you are waiting for something that I cannot provide."

Ludwig was quiet, processing what Elizabeth had written. He nodded, but his eyes showed his sadness.

"I understand, I should not have expected someone of your status to be so willing to give up your position to be with me."

Ludwig stood and walked to the door, holding it open for Elizabeth to leave. She put her hands together at her heart and felt her face turn hot again. Fighting back more tears, Elizabeth held his gaze before she left the apartment.

Chapter Twenty

July 1810

Maximilian waited on the front lawn of the estate. Elizabeth's grandmother watched from the window with a smile. Nicholas stood beside her. They watched Elizabeth approach Maximilian from the double doors at the front of the building.

"She seems to be warming up to him already," Nicholas whispered. "I do hope they get along, it has been difficult in the recent past."

"You were the same way with Olivia,

dear."

"I know, mother, but this is Elizabeth. She is much more stubborn than I."

~~~

Elizabeth clasped her hands together as she approached Maximilian. He turned toward her with a smile.

"Hello, Maximilian," Elizabeth said. He began walking in stride with her, in the direction of the lush garden on the north side of the grounds.

"Please, 'Max' is fine," he said. "How was your trip, Elise?"

"Long."

"Are you happy to be back in Germany?"

"I am happy to see Grandmother again."

The pair walked in silence for a bit. When

they reached the garden, Maximilian picked a cherry colored rose and handed it to Elizabeth.

"Thank you," she said. Her eyes grew sad suddenly.

"What is the matter?" Maximilian asked.

"I doubt you would understand, Maximilian."

"Just 'Max'. You can tell me, even if I do not understand."

"Well, I was looking forward to performing a duet with Herr Beethoven, but now that I am here I will not be granted the opportunity."

"That is a shame. I remember when Johann and I used to play, but now that he is passed I have not touched my violin in quite a while."

Elizabeth looked taken aback and she whipped her head to look at him.

"You play the violin?"

"Yes. Do you not remember when I started?"

She shook her head and he laughed.

"Yes, I began when we were children."

"I had no idea. You have never played for me before."

"Of course not. I did not want to embarrass myself in front of a beautiful woman."

"Will you play for me? Today?" Elizabeth asked, her voice showing excitement.

"Why don't we play together?"

"That sounds wonderful, Max."

Chapter

Twenty - One

May 1824

The chorus stood for the final movement of the symphony. The orchestra introduced the optimistic melody and built up the harmony for the vocalists to enter smoothly. The loud melodic line of the bass soloist acted like it was competing with the structured harmonies of the orchestra. The first chorus was dramatic and full, the singers spitting the crisp German words.

Flapping his arms like a bird in flight, Ludwig

marched the performers onward. Finding their breath where they could, the singers followed him with red faces and rounded lips. The piece seemed to pick up speed and finished in a frenzy.

The roar of a reverberation shook the performance hall and there was a pause before the audience lifted out of their chairs in applause. After a few seconds had passed, the contralto soloist placed her hands on the conductor's shoulders and turned the man around to face the audience.

Ludwig's hair was a mess of long swooping grey curls that flopped around his face as he bowed several times. He shook his head to move the loose strands out of his face. Without smiling, he recognized the performers and continued to bow.

~~~

Amongst the clapping, Maximilian leaned over close to Elizabeth's ear.

"He truly is a marvelous musician," he

said over the clapping. "If not the most marvelous of all time."

Elizabeth, never taking her eyes off the conductor, nodded in agreement. She watched him exit the stage.

"The most," she said. "The very greatest."

ABOUT THE AUTHOR

Zoe Garner wrote her first novel, *Elise,* while an undergraduate at Austin College with the help of her professor, Peter Anderson. A graduating senior with a Bachelor of Arts degree in English, she plans to continue her writing career.

88188318R00090

Made in the USA
Lexington, KY
08 May 2018